The Dancing Horn

Kenneth Rubangakene
Alicantorina Aluku

The Dancing Horn

Great Mystery at the Well

JustFiction Edition

Imprint

Any brand names and product names mentioned in this book are subject to trademark, brand or patent protection and are trademarks or registered trademarks of their respective holders. The use of brand names, product names, common names, trade names, product descriptions etc. even without a particular marking in this work is in no way to be construed to mean that such names may be regarded as unrestricted in respect of trademark and brand protection legislation and could thus be used by anyone.

Cover image: www.ingimage.com

Publisher:
JustFiction! Edition
is a trademark of
International Book Market Service Ltd., member of OmniScriptum Publishing Group
17 Meldrum Street, Beau Bassin 71504, Mauritius

ISBN: 978-620-0-49598-3

Chapter One

Luyomo, the hidden mystery

Part 1

Hahaaa…Hahaaa….Okang my boy!
My big boy raised in the great land
Of *Luyomo*,
The land that flows milk and honey
The Land of great mystery
The mystery hidden for years
From the entire world;

The great hope of the land is back
In full force on *Okang*'s feet
The feet of the King
King *Lakela* of *Painata*
The Champion of all Kingdom
Fierce and brave
Humble and lovely
Adored by all people of the land.

The sacred land
Hidden from the face of entire world
Not because it's aloof
But,
It was not time for it
To be revealed.

Why now?
Yes, *Ayaa*, the princes of the land
Of *Luyomo* is proud of her chiefdom,
Okang, the ruler of *Painata*
Is the cornerstone of the great w*ell*
The *well* of *Ocan Laguna*
Who was killed by his enemies,
Enemies of progress
Haters of love
Haters of better life
Because, they wish to continue
To live under same power
And fear of unknown;

I know he was a righteous-man
Though he doesn't speak any word
His presence in the land of *Luyomo*
Gave hope to us little *kittens*.

We still feel his presence
Though he is gone for years
His blood still feels our heart
Soften our minds, veins
And eyes,
Making us to see clearly
Through the mist of life.

We know it's time to reveal to *kittens*
The new race of people
Who grew in diversity of humanity
Taught and raise in a modern world
Mixed up of all caliber
Of atoned colors,

We believe, the spirit of *Ocan Laguna*
Is powerful, not so powerful as *Aluk*
Because she was killed in the same way
Not because she did anything wrong
But, because of the beauty of her hearts,
Body, soul and spirit,
The love for all people was the core
Of her life;

To see her shades while I was nine
For the last time was something
My mind can't get ride off,
The off of life
The only seed of *Painata*
Vanished in the swamp of *Wang Min Atube*
A fierce Well, I'm not so sure
But, I can feel her presence with us
The love, presence, care and compassion

The compassion of heart she had
Was so amazing she had to give her life
For me to come in;
The way I believe her departure
Open way for my birth
So that I can reveal to the world
The mystery of injustices in the land.

We couldn't believe it's 30years now
That no one ever thinks of her anymore
But, *kittens* must know *Aluk*
And *Ocan Laguna* are the piller
Of the land,
Oyoo the wisdom of *Luyomo*
The one who gave his life for us
So that we may have life
Life in full;

The fullness comes with patience,
Courage, hope and dignity
Peace, happiness, care
And compassion,
The compassion of reality
The reality of clear minds
Connected in one spirit
The spirit of Union,
Union of diversity
And forgiveness is what is up to;

No one in the land of *Luyomo*
Would have known the 3 hosts,
Courageous and lovely people
Who were killed in mystery,
The mystery kept sacred
For the gods,

Sacred till now
So that we might learn
To honor our heroes
Those who gave their life for humanity,
The one who served with love
The one who served our nations
From oppressors and injustices
Bad governance and inherit-ant
Hostile rules of law,

The law of racism and discrimination
The law of wealthy and poor
The law of villages and towns
The law of dehumanization
The law of elites and illiterate
The law of curse and reason
The law of corruption and war
The law of exploitation of workers
The law of man-made diseases
The law of dark hearted people
This is not what we want to see.

We love to see a world full of love
We love to see a world full of care
We love to see a world full of compassion
We love to see a world full of integrity
We love to see a world full of diversity
We love to see a world full of unity
We love to see a world full of equality
We love to see a world full of technology
Technology that brings positivity
Not hatred.

Part II

We know *Okang* grew up in knowledge
Of the old and new world
Kittens too had the same wisdom
But, that wisdom is so powerful
So powerful that they nearly forgot
Who they are;
But, that won't happen
Because,
Our grandfather, *Oola Wilson* is alive
Alive in spirit and exist
With us every day.

His departure
Gave us sorrows,
His suffering with pain before he left
This world,
Words cannot describe the pain,

I heard from a far land about him
But, I couldn't come on time
Not until, when he breathe his last.

To me, that is not a lost
Because,
His presence was seen in *Lanya –dyang*
A swamp of river heading *West*
Of the slopes of *Acholibur*
The holes of blacks,

The black road of fierce dews
In his house built for him
But, he never lived in
Because,
Kittens couldn't allow him in;

His LIFE is alive and always,
Because,
We know what he taught us
Will never vanish from the entire world,

The world of wicked people
The world of uncircumcised heart
The world of suffering community
The world of favourism
The world of unemployment
The world of racism
The world that separates elders, old people
And keep them in cage,

A cage of humans!

A cage of loneliness and separation
Separation from entire life
Separation from their family
Separation from their love ones
Separation from their friends
Separation from modern life
Separation from enjoyment
Separation from better care
And,
Making them to live like birds,
Being fed like birds
Being lifted like birds
Birds of the sea
Wondering on their won
And waiting for who will come
To their rescue

It's - not - enough
It's – not - enough
It's – not – enough…
.

.

To put them in cage!

Everyone needs freedom
Freedom of better life
Freedom of speech
Freedom of movement
Freedom of expression
Freedom of liberty
Freedom of reverence
Freedom of family life
And freedom of enjoyment,

But,
We know,
The *Kittens* world has changed everything.

They have changed what we used to be
They have brought in new things
The things we never thought of
The old lyric of music that flows
And goes to the heart is replaced,
Replaced with horror of no humor,

Respect has vanished
And disappeared from the world.

No one care for one another
Everyone care for themselves
No one sees love as intimacy
But,
As a source of money
And a way of life,

No one value marriage…!

Marriage has become a contract
Not a covenant,
A covenant assigned from the foundation
Of the world
By the Supreme Being
The creator of the entire Universe

No one value children….!

Children has become a burden to many
They see them as problems not treasure
They see them as nothing
Not even one would consider lifting
Lifting them up with love.

Some has no fear of killing them
Killing in the name of un-wanted,

What..?
Un-wanted..?

Millions of souls of little children
Are wondering and crying in tubes
Crying in dustbins
Crying in test tubes
And crying in rubbers,

No one care about life anymore…!

Life has become nothing to worry about
Kittens has put power to remove life
To remedy life
And call it advancement
In the new life,
Some had even gone too far
By diminishing co-existence
Through same sex-marriage
This will lead to no life in future
As there will be no reproduction
And co-creation in the right way
As designed by the Almighty
From the foundation of the world

The co-creation portal has become enormous
The future looks full of dooms
The universe is bleeding for lack of wisdom
The new trend has become new-normal
The normal has become new-world order,
The world were humans has become slave
Enslaved by themselves

A world of confusion and total darkness
Darkness of both heart and soul
No one care about life
Especially,
The wondering souls of innocent people
The one who gave their life
For our freedom

The freedom of human kind comes from heart
The freedom of human kind comes from body
The freedom of human kind comes from mind
And freedom of all life is important
None is more important than the other,
All is Life
And
Life is life;

However,
The new life of wounded *kittens*
Has given rise to ruthless world
That has No fear of Murder,
No fear of fornication
No fear of divorce
No fear of adultery
No fear of theft
No fear of helping one another with love
No fear of enslavement of innocent souls
Working many hours with little pay
And living in camps
In the name of safety…,

This never existed in the world we know,

Part III

We see all life equal
Everyone is the same
No matter who you are
And where you are from,

You can't see any form of discrimination
Disunity is punishable by death
Death on the cross
In the presence of entire community
Watching in awww....!

This is what I know
(Grand-pa voicing)

But, that won't help my *Okang*

I am old now,
And above all live in spirit world
But,
That doesn't stops me
From talking to you,

You are my grand-son,
The hair of the thrown
Thrown of wisdom and power
Your kingdom shall be blessed
With new ways of life
The life "I know"
And the life you will live is blessed,

(Okang bow down in front of grand-pa spirit)

So.....
By the power granted to me
By the mother goddess of *Luyomo*
Lapono, the Supreme Being
The keeper of the Universe
The healer of all sickness
Shall always be with you
Blessings upon you (recite it with me)
Blessings upon you
Blessings upon you
Blessings upon you
Blessings upon you
Blessings upon you
From the North- East
To the end of the world
Your kingdom shall never end
Go and rule with love
And meekness

Okang my boy
You are blessed,
Ayaa, the princes of the land of Luyomo
Her womb shall bear wisdom
The wisdom that never surface
On the entire world
With healing of great power
That no one shall touch the fruits
Of her womb,

That's fruit of new life
The life that shall rule entire Universe
With love, compassion and unity,

Also,
In that womb lies great treasure
The treasure of wealth
The treasure of inspirations
The treasure of eternity
Guarded by silver and gold
To bring hope to the world.

The womb shall bring joy to you
And all who bless you shall be blessed
And those who curse you shall be cursed,
Because,
The god mother of *Luyomo*
Is proud of her,
"I" am seeing blessing
And a new generation
Of great leaders
Who have calm mind
Full of love for all,

That love shall never disappear
From the face of the world,
"I" can see a humble race
Who love one another
Respect one another
And care as one community
Community of the Queen
The Queen of Okalma descent.

Chapter Two

At the Well of Lapono

Part I

At the *well*
We know the queen and her fruits
Has grown in power over the universe
North, East, South and West
The glimpse of entire world
Keep shining and glowing
Brightly in the sky
Amidst stars of all stars
Blue, red and gold
Where life could be
A source of wisdom,

Wisdom everyone is looking for
From the planet earth
The perception of Universe
Sealed from two faces
Of atmosphere,
There appeared from no where
Unexpected
Large bomb of knowledge
Falling from the sky
With sparkling lights
Of intense heat and pressure
Controlling the entire North and East,

While the real fact is that
South is dimmed
Which make it unbelievable
Of all,

And West looks different
The extinction of wild life
And insects has become a song
Worms and fish look glowing in waters
But,
Dies when out of it,

Seas claps in amazement
And happiness for carrying life
Not until
It dries up
That its value is seen
And when we see land, valleys
Mountains are shapes of the world

Created with great love
Affection and care by Him
Who are above all things
The one who ever lived
The one who is so merciful
So lovable
So meek
So powerful
So creative
So adorable
So generous
So gorgeous
So caring
And;
 So calm to listen to the voice,

The voice of our people who sacrifice their life
For this great land
Still remains in our hearts, body and soul.

The Dancing Horn   *Great Mystery*

We can smell them all around us everyday
We can feel their presence in the sky
We can feel their protection from enemies
We can feel their help in decision
We can feel their guide in day to day life
We can feel their sound in birds
We can feel their voice in animals
We can see them in our dreams
We can see them in our instincts
We can see them in our success
They are our power and source of wisdom

It takes a pure heart to see
The great wisdom of our ancestors
The great love they had for us
The great wealth and prosperity
The great secrets
Lost from the world

Yes, it takes determination to feel
Their presence.

You need clean heart and body
To draw near to them
And learn
The secrets of life…

I, *Okang,* know it
Because I was with them
The life no one will see
Except,
Them who lived in the spirit world
The world of power and wisdom
That no one can reach
Unless you have pure hearts,

A heart free from doubts
A heart free from racism
A heart free from curse
A heart free from bad thought
A heart free from any form of dirt
A heart free from hatred
And,
 A heart ready to learn and receive.

To receive wisdom and teachings from them
Who lived in the spirit world;
You need patience
You need perseverance to enter the dark well
You need courage to let go people in your life
You need love not lust
You need good attitude
And
Above all
You need an open heart
Ready to receive from divinity,

You can't receive anything without hope
The hope that things are not the same
Not the same the way we think
Not the same they are seen with our naked eyes
Not the same they appear in physical universe
The universe seen in lenses of vision

You need vision
Clear vision to see things in 3Ds
3Ds of life
Life that expand values
The compassion of reality
The reality of clear sense
Sense of humor
Real humor
Not fake like many do
To please earthly rulers
And Authority figures,

The 3Ds goes beyond normal vision
Clarity of life shown on top of the mountain
The mountain of great wealth
Wealth of wisdom
Wisdom can see truth
In the eyes
And lies in the words spoken,

Ever words counts to a life
Whether pure or not
But,
All is good for those who are ready
To receive from the divine world

The divine is not what you think
It's beyond human nature
And understanding
Because,
You need clarity and pure hearts
To see through,

The power of all who lived before us
Is what kept us all alive,
For without them
We have nothing to brag about,
Without them, we have no human race'
Without them, we are all nothing
A sand that can be blown by wind
And
Scattered in the air.

The air full of mist and warm
Its warmness is how we know our ancestors
Are presence with us,
And there is no doubt
You too can feel them
By closing your eyes
Focusing on spirituality
Calling them in your hearts, mind and soul
You will feel them coming,
Coming
Coming
And coming to your rescue

Part II

You can imagine a time with them
The one whom you thought were dead
But,
Alive in the spirit world
Not easy to describe
But,
Can't be kept sacred
Because it's time to make the world know
How powerful they could be,

I can feel their presence each time
I close my eyes
Walking among multitudes
They were all put inside
A room to allow me pass first
As the hero of the land of *Luyomo*
The most adored boy of Painata
The next hair of cirayi's thrown

I was given a stick inform of a spear
To go and promote our culture
All sings in adoration
Okang, the hair is back!
We are proud of you
"Man gang-wa"
"Man tekwaro-wa"
Keep sharing
Keep sharing
And let all people know it,

Reaching home with pride
All people were asleep
Not until, a hand appeared
And brought me a book
Put on my head
And said;
This book is *"hope"*
Keep promoting it
Keep promoting the word
And;
Write them on your forehead
And put them on your children's forehead
Write them on their hands
So that everyone knows
You are a king
 The ruler of this amazing land,

The land of "hope" for the entire world
The only point if discovered
And explore,
 Shall calm the world
You know it's possible
And will be a great place for humanity.

I have cleared the field
Went across the border point
Planted germinating seeds
 A sacred seed of life
That nobody has ever seen
The seed grew well in lines
Looking nice and healthy,

But remember,
Crossing borders of others is not a good thing
So, they asked me to plant other seedlings
And make demarcation,
However,
As I was making demarcation
Suddenly a steeply slopes appeared,
So sleeper
So sleeper
So sleeper
That no foot can get hold on it
Except those with power
Granted by the ancestors,

I was pushed down
And as I was falling down the slopes
My heart was almost losing breathe,
Fortunately and immediately
Appeared a shadow of human in front
Shadowing me from side to side
Covering me up.

And before I reach bottom of the hill
Appeared a pool of water
Diving inside like a leaf
Fully protected without knocking myself
On the stones of the sea,

Getting shock was incredible
Because,
 I had no idea swimming is.

As I struggle to get drawn
Appeared a huge tree
The tree of life
Hanging myself and lifting me up
With much love
As the waters sings;
Okang, the hero of the land of Luyomo
Okang, the hero of the land of Luyomo
Shall never die
Shall never die
Shall never die
He shall never die x2
Because the god mother of Luyomo
Lapono, is still sited on the thrown
And ruling with perfection.

Then she said, *(Lapono speaking to me)*

.

….

The spear handed to you is power
The power to lead *Luyomo* to her destiny
A destiny that no one sees
A destiny that no one had ever imagine
A destiny promised to your grandfather *Lakela*
A destiny promised to hairs of chiefdom
A destiny of pure love
A destiny that is sealed for many years
A destiny that will reign in unity
And love;

As long as "I" *Lopono*, the mother goddess
Of the land of *Luyomo* still live
There is nothing that will hurt you
There is nothing
Nothing
Nothing
Nothing
Nothing
Nothing
That shall hurt *my beloved Okang,*

Okang, The hero of the land of Luyomo
Okang, The hero of the land of Luyomo
Shall never die
Shall never die
Shall never die,

"I" *Lapono* and my guarded soldiers
Gave you power to overcome death
Even death on the cross.

Any enemy that tries to harm you
Shall harm themselves,
Any enemy that tries to hurt you
Shall hurt themselves
Any enemy that tries to stand on your way
Shall die on seeing your face
Any enemy that tries to block you
Shall vanish like morning dews
Any enemy that tries to deny you access
Shall have their ways blocked
Any enemy that tries to kill you
Shall kill themselves.

My wisdom, the chef of the goddess
Had been given to you.

You are my King
The next hair of the land of *Luyomo*

"I" have given it to you
Though no one has seen it
Because
You are mine forever.

"I" know,
They will try their best
To pull you down
As they did before you were born,
But,
That won't happen again;

"I' know,
My prince is now grown up
And
Has my power to cause lights go off
To ask and will be given
To open closed doors
To shut down doors of enemies
To open the destiny of my people
Which was locked for 30 years.

"I" know,
They won't be happy of my *Okang*
Because,
They poison you at birth
Will sickness that had no cure for 10years
But,
'I' *Lapono*, the mother goddess of the land
Of *Luyomo*,
Came down and show them
That,
My Okang shall never die
My Okang will live forever
To fulfill the mystery of *Painata,*
The great clan ruled by *Lakela*
And;
Dispersed by hypocrites
Who created hatred and fears
Among the peoples.

"I" *Lapono*, won't allow that to happen again.

It has come to time it up with meekness
The reign of my King – *Okang*
My King,
My Prince
And
My Love
Who is full of wisdom and integrity
Full of care for all people
Full of intimacy for everyone
Without any form of curse.

And;
 Ayaa, my princess is set beside you
She is my favorite of all women in this land
She is my choice
The choice of beauty done from spirit
And heart
In accordance to the will
The will of *Lakela*,
Our great grand-father
Who ruled with Love
"I" *Lapono* say,
Peace Be with You
Peace Be with You
Peace Be with You
Peace Be with You, always.

In this Waters
My tree appeared to save you from drowning
Because,
 "I" know "I' was with you always
"I" wanted you to know that,
"I" am with you
"I" am with you always.

You might be weary in this life
You might be discourage in this life
You might be forced to follow new rules
You might be forced to adjust
To others' traditions,
You might be called many names
You might be rejected
You might be arrested for no reason
You might be segregated because of color
You might be discriminated
You might be called illiterate
But,
As long as you remained in spirit
And follows all I taught you in spirit
There is no one who will stand in your way.

Your way shall be guarded with silver and gold
Your path shall be cemented with tarmac
Tarmac made from clouds
Clouds of mist
Full of sulpher.

Your house shall be sparkling with humor
Your room shall be protected by my people
Because,
"I" know,
You are my Prince
The Prince of the land of *Luyomo,*

Part III

The Prince
Taught by life
To live with love
And care for everyone
Without any discrimination,

"I" *Lapono*,
Knows you very well
You have power,
But,
Master these WORDs,

These are the WORDs of wisdom
WORDs that requires wisdom
And only those who have wisdom
Can understand
Understand the knowledge
And
The 10 COMMANDEMENT of Life
The pure secret of life,

Open your ears
And
Listen now
To
The **10 commandment of life**

[i]

Happiness is a gift
A gift of life that you can't find on the road
A gift of pure understanding
Built on humility and hope
Without fear of the unknown,
Remember,
Ruling a group needs good temper
Request power and be patient
People always support
No matter the truth

[ii]

Women are co-creator of life
They give life and make life exist
For without them
Life ceases to exist,
There are many type of these women
There are beautiful wife,
Just taking care of herself
And always in front of mirror.
There are good wife,
Gather family together
And respect her husband secrets.
There are smart wife,
They are looking for quality
And always arrogant
Because they are educated.
And lastly,
There are good mother wife,
They are not beautiful
But, ready to sacrifice for success of her family.

The Dancing Horn 🕊 *Great Mystery*

[iii]

Death is a natural phenomenon
It's uncontrollable
It's uncalled for
But,
If you want to die young
Get married when you don't have any resources
Because,
 For women, it's all about love
And it's a mandate of a man
To provide for the family

[iv]

Wickedness is something corrosive
It's explode like volcanoes
Destroying entire zones of the earth
But,
For those who are wicked to you
Leave them,
Set your own rules and principles
And
Stick to it without looking back,
By doing this,
You will conquer the world
Don't forget the world is full of wicked people

[v]

Wisdom is seeing what no one sees
Understanding what no one understands
For humanity, wisdom has become a problem
The wises people are those who have no
education,
The wises people always have lonely life
The wises people are the one who suffers more
The wises people are the kindest of all
Not just because they want to see
accompaniment,
But,
They wish not to let anyone go through
The same they did in life,
They take care of 4 basic elements of chemistry
Fire – *Head*
Air – *Chest*
Water – *Belly*
Land – *Legs*

[vi]

Love to tolerate an instinct
Because,
The more you show people that you know them,
The more you will be left alone
The more you are wise,
Your wisdom will kill you.
Never run after a person who is running away
Because of respect,
Give opportunity,
But, don't show that you are giving opportunity,
Why?
To avoid lying and hiding.
Encourage your kids to do what they like
And also show them what you think is good
For them.
Education is key to wisdom.
Tradition, cultures and modern life
Are path way to reaching greater wisdom.

[vii]

Ignorance is sometimes good
Because,
The more you know
The higher the pressure.
The greatest of a man comes when he sees better
But,
Still keeps the faith.
When someone doesn't refuse
Anything from you,
Don't ask everything from them

[viii]

Be kind
Give everybody whatever they ask.
Be good
Give people what is useful for them.
We all have one reason, the one thing
To be thankful for every day.
When you are with bad people, Be Kind
Accept their thoughts,
Apprehend them,
Encourage and support their ideas
And don't divert from their thoughts.
But,
When you are living with good people, Be Good
Talk to them according to their understanding
As long as you know what you are doing
Life is very easy

The Dancing Horn 🪽 *Great Mystery*

[ix]

Never put shame on any human being
Even if a person is your enemy
Revenge belongs to the almighty.
As long as you can do something for someone
Do it,
Never revenge,
And,
When you are disappointed - leave

[x]

Family is the smallest unit of life
In a family, you will have boys and girls
As a father, it's your responsibility
To teach and handle them with care
For boys, you have to be tough on them
Because,
They will spend over 40 years with you
For girls, you have to be linen, tough and lovely,
Feel confident
Because
Educating a girl, is educating a nation
Perverting a girl is perverting a nation.
Remember, we celebrate mothers when they are
alive
And,
Fathers when they are dead.
Don't forget,
You are a whole that exist to live a full life.

Chapter Three

The sacred gate of life

Part I

You are a whole being
A sacred gate to holiest of holies
Where life begins.

Life is always easy when you know
Where you are going,
If you have to make a choice
Don not love half lovers
Do not entertain half friends
Do not indulge in works of the half talented
Do not live half life
And
Do not die a half death.

If you choose silence, then be silent
When you speak, do so until you are finished
Do not silence yourself to say something
And do not speak to be silent,

If you accept to speak,
Then express it bluntly
Do not mask it.

If you refuse, then be clear about it
For an ambiguous refusal
Is,
But a weak acceptance.

Do not accept half solution
Do not belief half truths
Do not dream half dream
Do not fantasize about half hopes.

Half a drink will not quench your thirst
Half a meal wills not satiate your hunger
Half the way will get you no where
Half an idea will bear you no results
Your other half is not the one you love
It's you in another time
Yet in the same space,
It's you when you are not.

Half a life is a life you didn't live
A word you have not said
A smile you postponed
A love you have not had
A friendship you didn't know
To reach and not to arrive
To work and not work
And
Attend,
Only to be absent.

What really makes you stronger than them
Closest to you
And the stranger to you
Is,
The half,
The mere moment of Inability.

But,
You are able
Because
For you are not half being
You are a whole
The exist to live a life
Not,
Half a life

Part II

The sweetness of full life is hidden
The sensitivity of full life is like yoni flowers
They are the temple
And home of life
The knowledge and wisdom
The secrecy hidden for decades
'the w-o-m-a-n"

For her dot is the lips of love
That forms the entrance to the holiest
The guardians of the body
And soul;
They are the flowering sentinels
Who serve sacred well
And life force.

The message of honor
With qualities connected to souls
The qualities of welcoming new life
The qualities of safety
The qualities of trust
The qualities of praise
The qualities of appreciation
The qualities of connection to the web
Of life,
And the qualities of warmth
Plus wholesomeness,

It opens
The sacred gate like flowers
With praise and appreciation;
The honor to be recognized
Seen,
And welcomed by life.

This make her become a welcome portal
To any energy deem worthy of entrance
Respecting true self love.

Vulnerability and humility opens the doorway
To love and intimacy.
Without vulnerability and humility,
As well as appreciation, devotion
And trust,
The yoni can't open
And the grail womb cannot be entered.

Remember,
Intimacy is a mutual exchange
And,
In giving these qualities,
We receive them.

The entrance of yoni helps open us
Into deeper trust
Trust yourself
And what you are letting into you
Or
Choosing to keep out
The wounds,
Both personal and collective
All revolve around trust.

So,
For a m-a-n to come fully into you
They must approach with appreciation
Purity of heart and intent,
Completely honoring this sacred portal
Into the famine.
They must also feel welcomed
In order to enter with Peace.

For her to surrender
Into this space of trust
She must respect her m-a-n
Feel held safe and supported by him.
She must trust both his strength
And gentleness
As well as his ability to penetrate her with love.

Ofcourse,
She will not surrender
Or
Open this sacred gate
If she doesn't feel respected
And,
Appreciated from the m-a-n she is with
Because,
Her yoni is a divine passage
For the body and soul
The holder
The matrix of generation
The origin of life
The primal source of all creation
And,
Above all,
 The birth place of universe.

It's a temple gate where pure essence of life
Can be connected.

It's the opening into the holy womb
The birth place of humanity.

It's a great teacher
For w-o-m-e-n to learn true self love
Sovereignty and self-respect
By only welcoming into her
That, which is loving,
Trust worthy
And honors her essence,

The sacred doorway
Into new generation...

Table of contents